MOONGAME

FRANK ASCH

ALADDIN PAPERBACKS

Revised cover edition, 1999

Aladdin Paperbacks
An imprint of Simon & Schuster
Children's Publishing Division
1230 Avenue of the Americas
New York, NY 10020
Text copyright © 1984 by Frank Asch
20 19 18 17 16 15 14
Printed in the United States of America

The Library of Congress has cataloged a previous edition as follows:
Asch, Frank. Moongame
Summary: During a game of hide-and-seek, Moon hides behind a cloud, leaving his friend Bear very worried.
[Hide-and-seek—Fiction. 2. Animals—Fiction.
3. Moon—Fiction] I. Title.
PZ7.A778Mpf   1988 [E] 88-6572
ISBN 0-689-83518-3
(ISBN-13: 978-0-689-83518-6)

To Devin, Amanda, Rachel, Megan, Sam, Caleb,
Jeremy, Lindsey, Chris, Daniel, and Luke

One day, Little Bird showed Bear a new game:
hide and seek. First he told Bear to hide
and counted to ten: 1, 2, 3, 4, 5, 6, 7, 8, 9, 10.
Then he went looking for Bear.

"I found you!" chirped Little Bird when
  he found Bear hiding behind some bushes.
"Now it's your turn to find me!"
  All day long, until the sun went down,
  Bear and Little Bird played their new game.

That night when Bear was all alone he
looked up in the sky and said to the moon,
"Let's play hide and seek!
First I'll hide and you find me."

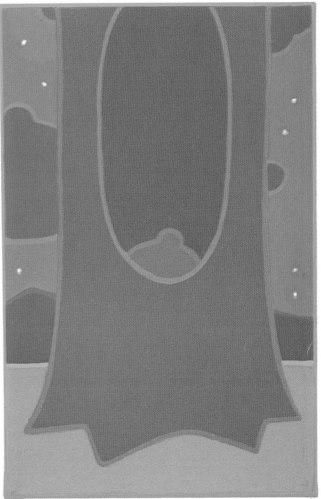

Then Bear ran as fast as he could
until he came to an old hollow tree.
Climbing inside, he ducked down
so the moon couldn't see him.

Bear waited for a while, then he poked his
head up. When he did, the moon was right
there looking down at him.
"Okay," said Bear, "you found me.
Now it's your turn to hide."
Closing his eyes, Bear began to count
just as Little Bird had shown him.

At that moment a gentle breeze

slowly hid the moon behind a big cloud.

When Bear finished counting, he set out
to find the moon. First he thought he
found the moon hiding behind some rocks.

Then he thought he found the moon
hiding in someone's house.

When Bear thought he found the moon hiding
in a tree he shook the tree and cried,
"I found you, Moon!"
But Bear was mistaken.
All he found was a big balloon.

Then Little Bird came by to visit.

"Will you help me find the moon?" asked Bear.

"Sure, I'll help," chirped Little Bird.

Bear and Little Bird looked and looked

but they couldn't find the moon.

So they went to the forest to ask for help.

"I think the moon is lost," explained Bear.

"Can you help me find him?"

"Don't worry, we'll help you,"
 replied the animals in the forest.

Together they searched and searched.

But they couldn't find the moon.

At last, Bear sat down and sighed,

"The moon is lost, and it's all my fault!"

Then Bear got an idea.

He jumped up and cried,

"Okay, Moon, I give up. You win!"

Just then the breeze began to blow again,

and the moon came out of its hiding place.

"Look," chirped Little Bird, "The moon wasn't lost.
He was just hiding behind that big cloud."
Bear was so happy he danced and danced.

Then everyone played hide and seek.